W9-CSY-586

MOUSE'S BIRTHDAY

MOUSE'S BIRTHDAY

Jane Yolen

ILLUSTRATED BY
Bruce Degen

G.P. Putnam's Sons · New York

Text copyright © 1993 by Jane Yolen
Illustrations copyright © 1993 by Bruce Degen
All rights reserved. This book, or parts thereof, may not be reproduced
in any form without permission in writing from the publisher.
G. P. Putnam's Sons, a division of The Putnam & Grosset Group, 200 Madison Avenue,
New York, NY 10016. G. P. Putnam's Sons, Reg. U.S. Pat. & Tm. Off.
Sandcastle Books and the Sandcastle logo are trademarks belonging to
The Putnam & Grosset Group. First Sandcastle Books edition 1995.
Published simultaneously in Canada. Printed in Hong Kong.
Text design by Colleen Flis. Hand-lettering by David Gatti.
The text is set in Kennerley.
Library of Congress Cataloging-in-Publication Data

Yolen, Jane. Mouse's birthday/Jane Yolen;
illustrated by Bruce Degen. p. cm.
Summary: One after another, several animals try to squeeze into
Mouse's very small house to help him celebrate his birthday.
[1. Mice—Fiction. 2. Animals—Fiction. 3. Birthdays—Fiction.
4. Stories in rhyme.] I. Degen, Bruce, ill. II. Title.
PZ8.3.Y76Mo 1993 [E]—dc20 92-15291 CIP AC
ISBN (hardcover) 0-399-22189-1
3 5 7 9 10 8 6 4
ISBN (Sandcastle) 0-399-22845-4
1 3 5 7 9 10 8 6 4 2
First Impression

Happy Birthday!
To David Morrison—July 24th and
Catriona Morrison—September 18th
—J.Y.

For all the Steins of Tapscott Street
—B.D.

Mouse's house is very small,

Very small,

Very small.

Hardly any room at all
For anyone but Mouse.

In comes Cat upon his knees,
Carrying a gift of cheese,
Trying very hard to squeeze
Into Mouse's house.

In comes Dog upon his knees,
Carrying a pot of teas,
Trying very hard to squeeze
Into Mouse's house.

In comes Cow upon her knees,
Carrying a bowl of peas,
Trying very hard to squeeze
Into Mouse's house.

To MOUSE
from HORSE

In comes Horse upon his knees,
Carrying a pair of skis,
Trying very hard to squeeze
Into Mouse's house.

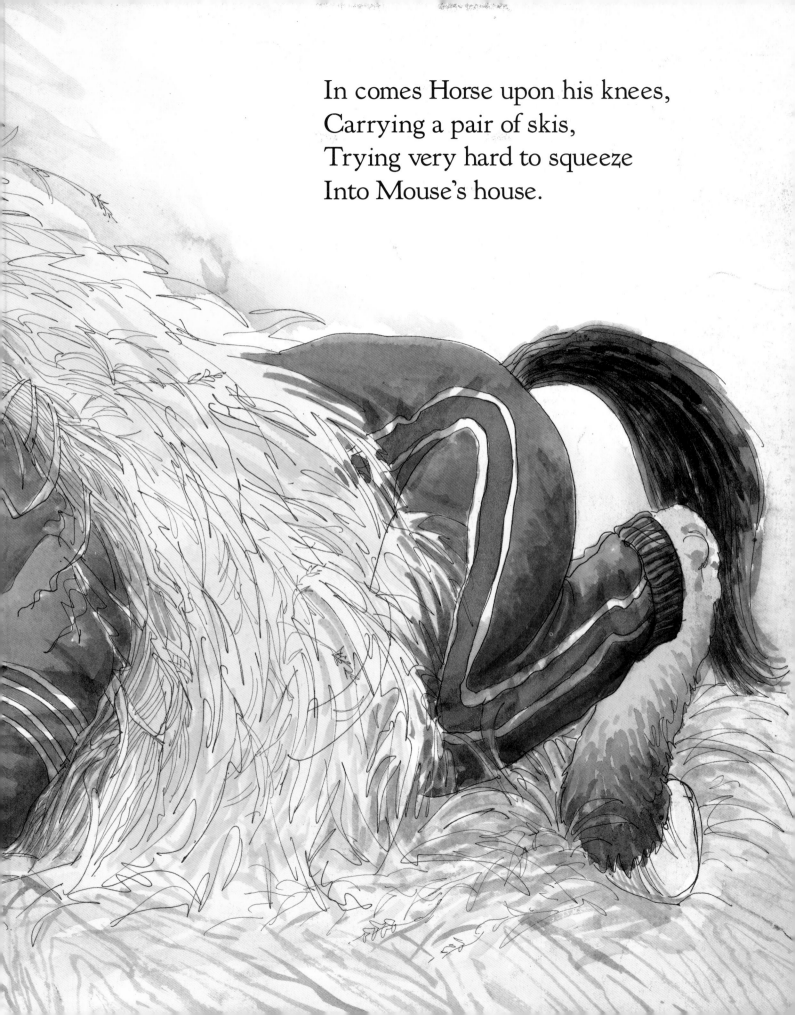

In comes Farmer on his knees,
Carrying a brown valise,
Trying very hard to squeeze
Into Mouse's house.

They all fit.
Candle's lit.
HAPPY BIRTHDAY, MOUSE.

Candle glows.

Mouse blows.

House goes.
WHOOOOOOOOOOOOOOOOOOSH!

Mouse's *new* house is very wide,
Very wide,
Very wide.
Everyone can fit inside.
Including little Mouse.

Pourroy